Big Pig
and
Little Pig

Cerdo
y
Cerdito

Big Pig
and Little Pig

David McPhail

Cerdo
y Cerdito

Green Light Readers   Colección Luz Verde

sandpiper

Houghton Mifflin Harcourt

Boston   New York   2009

"I am hot," said Big Pig.

—Tengo calor —dijo Cerdo.

"Me, too," said Little Pig.

—Yo también —dijo Cerdito.

"I am going to make a pool,"
said Big Pig.

—Voy a hacer una piscina
—dijo Cerdo.

"Me, too," said Little Pig.

—Yo también —dijo Cerdito.

"I am going to dig a hole,"
said Big Pig.

—Voy a hacer un agujero
—dijo Cerdo.

"Me, too," said Little Pig.

—Yo también
—dijo Cerdito.

"I am going to get a bucket,"
said Big Pig.

—Voy a traer un cubo
—dijo Cerdo.

"Me, too," said Little Pig.

—Yo también
—dijo Cerdito.

"I am going to fill up the pool," said Big Pig.

—Voy a llenar la piscina —dijo Cerdo.

"Me, too," said Little Pig.

—Yo también —dijo Cerdito.

"Now I can sit back down,"
said Big Pig.

—Ahora me puedo tirar al agua
—dijo Cerdo.

"Me, too!" said Little Pig.

—¡Yo también! —dijo Cerdito.

Let's Dig In!

Make Big Pig's favorite snack.

WHAT YOU'LL NEED

bread

big cookie cutter
little cookie cutter

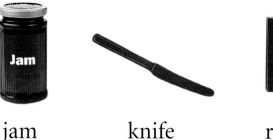

jam   knife   raisins

 Cut a big circle and a little circle in your bread with the cookie cutters.

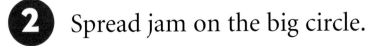 Spread jam on the big circle.

3 Cut one of the little circles in half. You'll use them for ears.

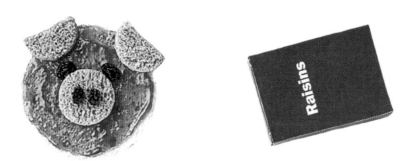

4 Make a pig face. Use raisins for the eyes and nostrils.

Write a sentence about your favorite snack. Share your sentence and your snack with a friend!

¡Vamos a Hincarle el Diente!

Haz la merienda favorita de Cerdo.

pan

cortador de galletas grande
cortador de galletas pequeño

mermelada

cuchillo

pasas

 Corta tres círculos en las rodajas de pan, uno grande y dos pequeños. Usa el cortador de galletas.

 Unta mermelada en el círculo grande.

3 Corta un círculo pequeño en dos mitades. Las usarás como orejas.

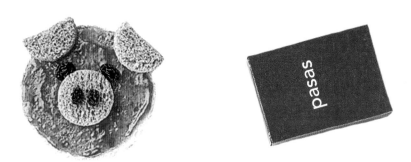

4 Haz una cara de cerdo. Usa pasas para los ojos y el hocico.

Escribe una frase sobre tu merienda favorita. ¡Comparte tu frase y tu merienda con un amigo o amiga!

Meet the Author-Illustrator

Te presentamos al autor e ilustrador

David McPhail

David McPhail loves to draw pigs. When he was a child, his favorite character was the pig in the book *Charlotte's Web*. "Pigs tickle me," he says. "They're fun because they do such silly things!" He hopes you giggled when you read *Big Pig and Little Pig*!

A David McPhail le encanta dibujar cerdos. Cuando era niño, su personaje favorito era el cerdo del cuento *Las telarañas de Carlota*. "Los cerdos me hacen gracia," dice. "¡Son divertidos porque hacen cosas muy tontas!" comenta. ¡David espera que te hayas reído al leer *Cerdo y Cerdito*!

Know the Translators
Conoce a las traductoras

F. Isabel Campoy and Alma Flor Ada are the authors of many books for children. They also love to translate them!

F. Isabel Campoy y Alma Flor Ada son autoras de muchos libros para niños. También les encanta traducirlos.

www.sandpiperbooks.com

First Green Light Readers edition 2001
Green Light Readers is a registered trademark of Houghton Mifflin Harcourt Publishing Company.

SANDPIPER and the SANDPIPER logo are trademarks of Houghton Mifflin Harcourt Publishing Company.

The Library of Congress has cataloged an earlier edition as follows:
McPhail, David M.
Big Pig and Little Pig/by David McPhail.
p. cm.
"Green Light Readers."
Summary: Although they like different things, Big Pig and Little Pig enjoy spending time together.
[I. Pigs—Fiction. 2. Friendship—Fiction.] I. Title. II. Green Light reader.
PZ7.M2427Bi 2001
[E]—dc21 00-9725
ISBN 978-0-15-206555-3
ISBN 978-0-15-206561-4 (pb)

A C E G H F D B
A C E G H F D B (pb)

Ages 4-6
Grades: K-1
Guided Reading Level: B-D
Reading Recovery Level: 4-5

Green Light Readers
For the reader who's ready to GO!

"A must-have for any family with a beginning reader."—*Boston Sunday Herald*

"You can't go wrong with adding several copies of these terrific books to your beginning-to-read collection."—*School Library Journal*

"A winner for the beginner."—*Booklist*

Five Tips to Help Your Child Become a Great Reader

1. Get involved. Reading aloud to and with your child is just as important as encouraging your child to read independently.

2. Be curious. Ask questions about what your child is reading.

3. Make reading fun. Allow your child to pick books on subjects that interest her or him.

4. Words are everywhere—not just in books. Practice reading signs, packages, and cereal boxes with your child.

5. Set a good example. Make sure your child sees YOU reading.

Why Green Light Readers Is the Best Series for Your New Reader

• Created exclusively for beginning readers by some of the biggest and brightest names in children's books.

• Reinforces the reading skills your child is learning in school.

• Encourages children to read—and finish—books by themselves.

• Offers extra enrichment through fun, age-appropriate activities unique to each story.

• Incorporates characteristics of the Reading Recovery® program used by educators.

• Developed with Harcourt School Publishers and credentialed educational consultants.

Colección Luz Verde
¡Para los lectores que están listos para AVANZAR!

"A must-have for any family with a beginning reader."—*Boston Sunday Herald*

"You can't go wrong with adding several copies of these terrific books to your beginning-to-read collection."—*School Library Journal*

"A winner for the beginner."—*Booklist*

Cinco sugerencias para ayudar a que su niño se vuelva un gran lector

1. Participe. Leerle en voz alta a su niño, o leer junto con él, es tan importante como animar al niño a leer por sí mismo.

2. Exprese interés. Hágale preguntas al niño sobre lo que está leyendo.

3. Haga que la lectura sea divertida. Permítale al niño elegir libros sobre temas que le interesen.

4. Hay palabras en todas partes, no sólo en los libros. Anime a su niño a practicar la lectura leyendo carteles, anuncios e información, como en las cajas de cereales.

5. Dé un buen ejemplo. Asegúrese de que su niño vea que USTED lee.

Por qué esta serie es la mejor para los lectores que comienzan

- Ha sido creada exclusivamente para los niños que empiezan a leer, por algunos de los más brillantes e importantes creadores de libros infantiles.

- Refuerza las habilidades de lectura que su niño está aprendiendo en la escuela.

- Anima a los niños a leer libros de principio a fin, por sí solos.

- Ofrece actividades de enriquecimiento, entretenidas y apropiada para la edad del lector, cuadas para cada cuento.

- Incorpora características del programa Reading Recovery usado por educadores.

- Ha sido desarrollada por la división escolar de Harcourt y por consultores educativos acreditados.